Keeping i...

Contents

Introduction	2
Long Ago	4
Mail	6
Telephone Talk	8
Telephone Text	10
Radio	12
Television	14
Going Online	16
Satellites	18
Newspapers	20
Keeping in Touch	22
Index	24

Introduction

There are many reasons why people keep in touch. They need to communicate with their family and friends. They also need to find information.

How are the people in the pictures communicating and finding information?

Long Ago

Long ago, keeping in touch wasn't easy. In some places, town criers called out the news. People also used ponies to carry the mail. Some people even used pigeons to carry messages.

Mail

People have communicated by mail for hundreds of years. Today, a lot of mail is carried by plane. Letters and postcards can travel across the world and be delivered in just a few days.

Telephone Talk

Talking on the telephone is one of the most popular ways of communicating. Today, people can stay in touch by phone from almost anywhere on Earth.

Early telephones looked very different from the phones of today. Now there are phones for homes, phones for cars, and phones to carry in your pocket.

Telephone Text

The telephone system isn't just for talking. It can be used to send words and pictures.

With a fax machine, you can send whole pages of information in just minutes!

Telephone connection

Sending text messages by phone is a quick way to keep in touch. These messages are usually very short.

Radio

For more than 80 years, people have listened to the radio for information and entertainment. We can turn on the radio at any time to listen to music or catch up on the latest news.

Before television was invented, families would gather around the radio every night.

Radios come in all shapes and sizes. Some have a clock in them.

Television

With television, we can see the news as it happens. We can watch live sports and concerts at home, too.

Early televisions could show only black and white pictures.

Going Online

Many people use computers for communicating and for finding information. They use e-mail for sending and receiving messages. They use the Internet for finding all kinds of information about our world.

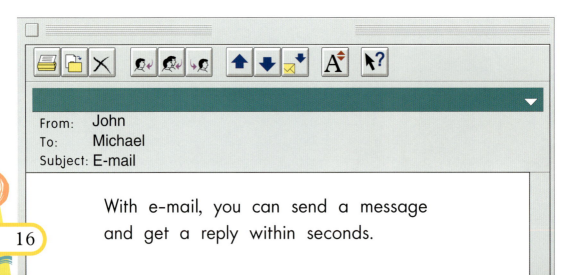

With e-mail, you can send a message and get a reply within seconds.

If you don't have a computer at home, there are other places where you can use the Internet.

Do You Know?

Now that e-mail is so common, ordinary mail is sometimes called snail mail!

Satellites

Satellites send pictures and sounds around the world in seconds. Signals travel from Earth to a satellite, and the satellite "bounces" the signals back down to Earth.

Satellite dishes are often located in deserts where they can send and receive clear signals.

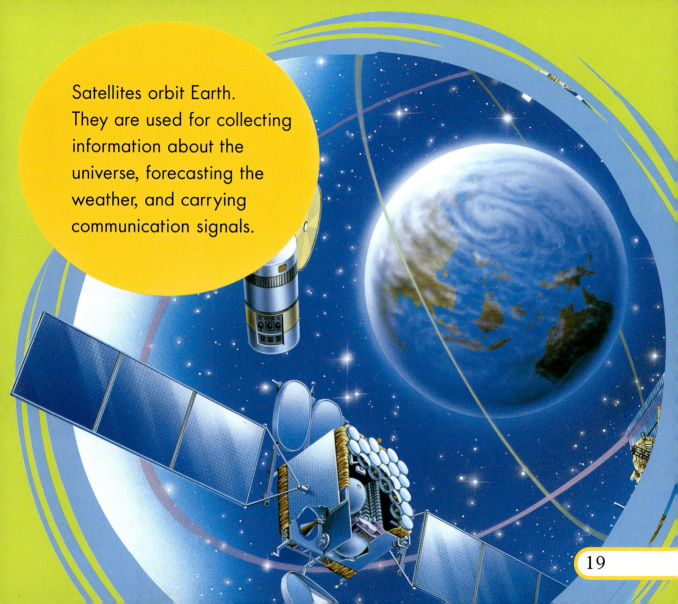

Satellites orbit Earth. They are used for collecting information about the universe, forecasting the weather, and carrying communication signals.

Newspapers

Newspapers have been around for much longer than telephones, radios, televisions, and computers. They are still very important today. Newspapers give us world and local news every day — and we can read them anywhere!

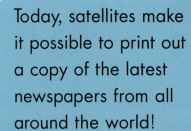

Today, satellites make it possible to print out a copy of the latest newspapers from all around the world!

Keeping in Touch

Most of the people in this picture are keeping in touch. How many ways of keeping in touch can you see?

Index

computers	16–17, 20
e-mail	16–17
Internet	16–17
mail	4, 6–7, 17
newspapers	20–21
pigeons	4
ponies	4–5
radio	12–13, 20
satellites	18–20
telephones	8–11, 20
television	14–15, 20
town criers	4